STAR & STRIPE
★Grand Opening!★

written by M. J. Offen

illustrated by Ruth Bennett

PIXEL✛INK

NEW YORK

PIXEL✚INK

Text copyright © 2022 by M. J. Offen
Illustrations copyright © 2022 by Ruth Bennett
All rights reserved
Pixel+Ink is a division of TGM Development Corp
Printed and bound in November 2021 at C&C Offset, Shenzhen, China.
Book design by Whitney Manger
www.pixelandinkbooks.com

Library of Congress Cataloging-in-Publication Data
Names: Offen, M. J., author. | Bennett, Ruth (Ruth Ellen), illustrator.
Title: Grand opening! / written by M. J. Offen ; illustrated by Ruth Bennett.
Description: First edition. | New York : Pixel+Ink, [2022] | Series: Star &
Stripe | Audience: Ages 4-7. | Audience: Grades K-1. | Summary: A
brother and sister lock horns and hold hooves as they work together to
build a food truck business in their town.
Identifiers: LCCN 2021014211 (print) | LCCN 2021014212 (ebook) | ISBN
9781645950103 (hardback) | ISBN 9781645951001 (ebook)
Subjects: CYAC: Brothers and sisters—Fiction. | Food trucks—Fiction. |
Cooperativeness—Fiction. | Cows—Fiction. | LCGFT: Picture books.
Classification: LCC PZ7.1.O375 Gr 2022 (print) | LCC PZ7.1.O375 (ebook) |
DDC [E]—dc23
LC record available at https://lccn.loc.gov/2021014211
LC ebook record available at https://lccn.loc.gov/2021014212

HC ISBN 978-1-64595-010-3
eBook ISBN 978-1-64595-100-1
First edition
1 3 5 7 9 10 8 6 4 2

For Mama, who taught me I could cook up anything I wanted to.—M.O.

For Mum and Dad, thank you for always being so supportive
and encouraging me to follow my dreams.—R.B.

This is Star. She's a cow.
Star is fancy.
Star is brainy.

This is Stripe. He's a bull.
Stripe is messy.
Stripe is goofy.

They're brother and sister and best friends, even though they disagree—*a lot.*

When they BUTT HEADS, things always go wrong.

But when they HOLD HOOVES, great things happen!

One thing Star and Stripe agree on is their favorite food: GRASSBURGERS! Just like Mama used to make.

All their friends and neighbors came to Mama's barbecues. Little Star and Stripe helped out.

They loved the company as much as the food.
Star and Stripe dreamed that one day they'd have
their own grassburger restaurant.

So they saved up their *moo*-lah until they had enough to start their restaurant!

Star wanted it to be downtown.

Stripe wanted it at the beach.

They butted heads. But they agreed to hop on their bike to look for just the right place.

They kept arguing though,
and didn't see the pothole.

They landed smack on their RUMP ROASTS!

COW PATTIES!

Star blamed Stripe: "Who ever heard of a steer who can't steer?"
Stripe blamed Star: "At least I'm not a cow having a cow!"

Luckily, old Mr. Slappytail was passing by in his food truck.
He stopped to lend a helping paw—and his tools.

Star and Stripe agreed to hold hooves and work together to fix their bike.

They changed their flat.

They collected their coins.

Done!
They gave each other
a HIGH HOOF.

That's when they saw the FOR SALE sign.
It turns out, after years serving customers all over Critter City,
Mr. Slappytail was retiring!

Star and Stripe had an idea:
Are moo thinking what I'm thinking?
   A restaurant on wheels could go downtown, the beach—anywhere!
They made Mr. Slappytail an offer to buy his food truck.
   SOLD!

Just like that, Star and Stripe
owned their very own restaurant.
They agreed the first thing
the food truck needed was a makeover.

Star wanted stars.
Stripe wanted stripes.

They were at it again, butting heads!
So they weren't paying attention when...

CRASH!

SPLASH!

Cow patties! What a mess!
Star blamed Stripe.
Stripe blamed Star.

They quarreled.
They quibbled.

Then they realized they hadn't eaten all day.
Star and Stripe weren't angry. They were HANGRY!

They agreed to hold hooves
and make something to eat,
THEN fix the paint job.

What would their first meal in the food truck be?
GRASSBURGERS of course!

Stripe mowed the grass.   Star made the patties.

Stripe flipped the burgers.
Star warmed the buns.

VOILA! Their first batch of grassburgers hot off the grill.
But would they taste as good as Mama's?

High hoof! GRASSTASTIC!
  While they ate, they looked at their truck.
  The red paint reminded them of when they were calves.
Star and Stripe had another idea:
Are moo thinking what I'm thinking?

They got straight to work.

Star and Stripe's BURGER BARN was ready to roll!

Now they just needed one thing: CUSTOMERS!

Star suggested the Art Mooseum, but snooty critters just turned up their noses.

Stripe suggested Badger Stadium during a hoofball game,
but *those* critters only wanted veggie dogs.

They heard:

"We **just** ate."

"Is the grass **organic?**"

"I **only** eat meat."

Nobody ordered—except one small mole.
And he only wanted a glass of water.

What a COWTASTROPHE!

Star and Stripe were worried. How would they get customers?
Star said they should advertise.
Stripe said they should give out free samples.

Star liked her idea best.
Stripe liked his idea best.
They butted heads—again.

They were so busy arguing,
they forgot they'd left the grill on!

Once again, holding hooves saved their hides! They were so relieved, they felt like celebrating. Which gave Star and Stripe their best idea yet.... They'd have a GRAND OPENING and invite all of Critter City!

Star made flyers.
Stripe made sliders.

Star drew a sign.
Stripe hung it high.

Star drove all over town, while Stripe gave out the flyers. Then there was nothing left to do but wait.

The big moment arrived. Would anyone come?

Star and Stripe threw open the shutters to find a line of critters as far as the eye could see.

CUSTOMERS!

Everyone loved their grassburgers and wanted seconds.
And thirds. And fifteenths.
From that day on, Star and Stripe's mobile Burger Barn was a hit.
HIGH HOOF!

It wasn't easy, but Star and Stripe made their dream come true!
Star said it was thanks to Stripe's skills on the grill.
Stripe said it was thanks to Star's fancy fliers.
They almost butted heads over who helped most,
then remembered what Mama says:
They're better together, like ketchup and mustard.
So they held hooves and shook on a job WELL-DONE!